Zink the Zebra

~ A Special Tale ~

To all the volunteers who have given their time,
expertise, and support to make the vision of
Zink the Zebra Foundation, Inc., a reality.
— L.W.

For a free color catalog describing Gareth Stevens' list
of high-quality books and multimedia programs,
call 1-800-542-2595 (USA) or 1-800-461-9120 (Canada).
Gareth Stevens Publishing's Fax: (414) 225-0377.

Special thanks to the employees of Precision Color Graphics of New Berlin, Wisconsin,
for donating the scanning and filmwork for *Zink the Zebra*.

Library of Congress Cataloging-in-Publication Data

Weil, Kelly.
Zink the zebra: a special tale / story by Kelly Weil; art by Jay Jocham.
p. cm.
Summary: Zink is different from other zebras, including her
brother Fink, because she has spots instead of stripes,
but her parents reassure her that she is not weird.
ISBN 0-8368-1626-9 (lib. bdg.)
[1. Zebras—Fiction. 2. Individuality—Fiction.
3. Brothers and sisters—Fiction.] I. Jocham, Jay, ill. II. Title.
PZ7.W4325Zi 1996
[E]—dc20 96-26693

This edition first published in 1996 by
Gareth Stevens Publishing
1555 North RiverCenter Drive, Suite 201
Milwaukee, Wisconsin 53212 USA

Text © 1995 by Zink the Zebra Foundation, Inc.
Illustrations © 1995 by Zink the Zebra Foundation, Inc.

Managing Editor: Patricia Lantier-Sampon
Art Director: Karen Knutson
Designer: Helene Feider
Production Manager: Susan Ashley
Editorial assistant: Diane Laska

Printed in the United States of America

2 3 4 5 6 7 8 9 03 02 01 00 99

Zink the Zebra
-A SPECIAL TALE-

Story by Kelly Weil
Paintings by Jay Jocham
Edited by Susan Rensberger

Gareth Stevens Publishing
MILWAUKEE

Once upon a time,
a zebra named Zink
lived in the Lipis Jungle
with her mother, her father,
and her brother Fink.

Zink was a normal
zebra in every way.
She had four legs, two ears,
one nose, one mouth,
one tail . . .

and spots.

All the other zebras
— even her mother, father,
and brother — had stripes.

Because Zink had spots,
the other zebras
wouldn't play with her.

Because the other zebras had
stripes, they thought
Zink looked odd.

One day Fink said to Zink,
"Why do you have spots?
They're so weird."

Zink said to Fink,
"Why do you have stripes?
They're so weird."

Zink and Fink couldn't
decide who was right.

No one in the Lipis Jungle
seemed to have
the answer.

Finally Zink and Fink
went home
to ask their parents.

"Which one of us is weird?"
they asked.

"Neither of you,"
their parents said.

"Whatever you are
is what you are,"
said their mother.

"We're all different,"
said their father.

"Being different
makes you special."

Then everyone nuzzled . . .

and Zink and Fink
went out to play.

The End

-About the Author -

Kelly Weil (1982 – 1993) was a little girl, like any other, who loved friends, family, books, swimming, animals, and computers — except at age eleven, she lost her battle with cancer. Kelly's story, *Zink the Zebra*, expresses the pain associated with the withdrawal of friendships due to misconceptions about human differences. The sensitive message Kelly relays concerns the importance of friendship, tolerance, and acceptance by others.

-About the Artist -

To Annalissa, may she continue to grow healthy and happy. — J.J.

Wisconsin native Jay Jocham's experiences as a boy vacationing in wild places and tromping through the farms and fields near his family's home influenced his dedication to conservation. A lifetime passion for wildlife has also inspired Jay to use his artistic talents to portray the unique beauty of the world's animals as well as their hardships and possible endangerment.

Recognized for his colorful and imaginative representations of animals and their habitats, this award-winning artist invites viewers to share his concern for wildlife. Through the sale of original art and limited-edition prints, he has helped fund programs to conserve wildlife and protect their habitats.

Jay lives with his wife and daughter amidst towering white pines near a spring-fed trout stream in central Wisconsin. Jay hopes his images of Zink the Zebra have listened to Kelly's quiet voice and have transformed her love of animals into a story of inspiration and hope.

-Note to Librarians, Parents, Teachers -

The truth is, we are more alike as human beings than we are different. Yet, too often, it is the small differences that are brought to children's attention, leading to judgments based on a person's outward appearance or perceived differences rather than his or her character or heart. Without understanding, hurtful things are said and done, sometimes scarring children for years — or even for a lifetime.

Written before she died of cancer in 1993, *Zink the Zebra* may explain how eleven-year-old author Kelly Weil perceived she was judged by others. Unfortunately, the judgments were often based on their fear of cancer or not knowing how to handle the changes in appearance that come with chemotherapy and other medical treatments. For Kelly, social rejection seemed to hurt more than her treatments.

Kelly's story communicates a powerful message of "special and different." Lovable Zink represents everyone perceived by others as different and is a role model that encourages children to be compassionate, accepting individuals. Beautiful artwork illustrates this simple but important story.

As children become aware of individual differences, they need guidance and understanding. This book is a useful tool that educators, parents, and grandparents can use when discussing sensitive topics, such as illness, physical and mental challenges, religious preferences, and racism. It is particularly suitable for students, preschool through eighth grade. Educational programs for any area or city are available from Zink the Zebra Foundation, Inc.

– Zink the Zebra Foundation, Inc. –

Zink the Zebra Foundation, Inc. took its name from Kelly Weil's compassionate story. Zink, a spotted zebra, represents everyone with differences that set them apart. The message encompasses lessons of tolerance and respect for diversity (racial, religious, economic) and for differences (physical or perceived) that might prompt negative attention. Like Zink, anyone with differences needs understanding, respect, compassion, and, above all, acceptance. These life skills need to be learned by children early in the educational process to make a real difference in their futures and in the futures of our communities.

To encourage development of these skills, Zink the Zebra Foundation, Inc. has created model programs for schools and community organizations. Its "Special and Different Education Program" is a series of dynamic, grade-specific (K-8), classroom educational modules with an entertaining and upbeat format. The Foundation also has collaborated with the Girl Scouts of Milwaukee Area (Wisconsin) to introduce the Zink the Zebra Patch program. A similar program is being developed with the Milwaukee County Council of the Boy Scouts of America. In collaboration with local theater companies, the Foundation has developed the play *Zink: the Myth, the Legend, the Zebra* as another medium for reaching young people with its message. All of these programs are available to any area of the country.

To learn more about the Foundation and/or programs for your area, please contact:

Zink the Zebra Foundation, Inc.
5150 N. Port Washington Rd., Suite 151
Milwaukee, WI 53217
(414) 963-4484   Fax: (414) 963-1598

Zink the Zebra, A Special Tale is available in two editions. A deluxe, jacketed edition can be ordered through Zink the Zebra Foundation, Inc. (Current price: $19.95, plus postage and handling.) All proceeds fund the work of the Foundation.

A library-bound edition can be purchased from Gareth Stevens, Inc. (See the address on the imprint page of this book.)

- More Books to Read -

Being Me. Life Education (series). Alexandra Parsons (Franklin Watts)

Friendly Differences. Mona Gansberg Hodgson (Concordia Publishing House)

Ian's Walk: A Story about Autism. Laurie Lears (Albert Whitman & Co.)

I'm Like You, You're Like Me: A Child's Book about Understanding and Celebrating Each Other. Cindy Gainer (Free Spirit)

Just Kids: Visiting a Class for Children with Special Needs. Ellen B. Senisi (Dutton)

People with Disabilities. What Do You Know About (series). Pete Sanders and Steve Myers (Franklin Watts)

Short Stature: From Folklore to Fact. First Books — Different from Birth (series). Elaine Landau (Franklin Watts)

Zink. Cherie Bennett (Delacorte Press)

- Videos -

The Amazing Children. (Bridgestone Multimedia)

The Dr. C & Elwood Show. (Samuel R. Caron, Ph.D., 226 N. Canyon, Sierra Vista, AZ 85635)

What Am I, Chopped Liver? Communicating with Your Doctor. (The STARBRIGHT Foundation)

Whitewash. (First Run Features)

Why, Charlie Brown, Why? A Story about What Happens When a Friend Is Very Ill. (Paramount Studios)

Zink: The Myth, the Legend, the Zebra (Based on the original concept Zink the Zebra, by Kelly Weil). Cherie Bennett (Zink the Zebra Foundation, Inc.)

- Web Sites -

Zink the Zebra. (www.zinkthezebra.org)

Band-Aides & Blackboards. (funrsc.fairfield.edu/~jfleitas/contents.html)

OncoLink: Kid's Corner. (oncolink.upenn.edu/resources/kids/index.html)

Team Harmony Student Corner. (www.teamharmony.org/corner.htm)

Due to the dynamic nature of the Internet, some web sites stay current longer than others. To find additional web sites, use a reliable search engine with one or more of the following keywords: *diversity*, *special needs*, *disabilities*, *differences*, and *illness*.